D1401081

STOP THAT NOISE!

PAUL GERAGHTY

HARCOURT BRACE & COMPANY

Orlando   Atlanta   Austin   Boston   San Francisco   Chicago   Dallas   New York
Toronto   London

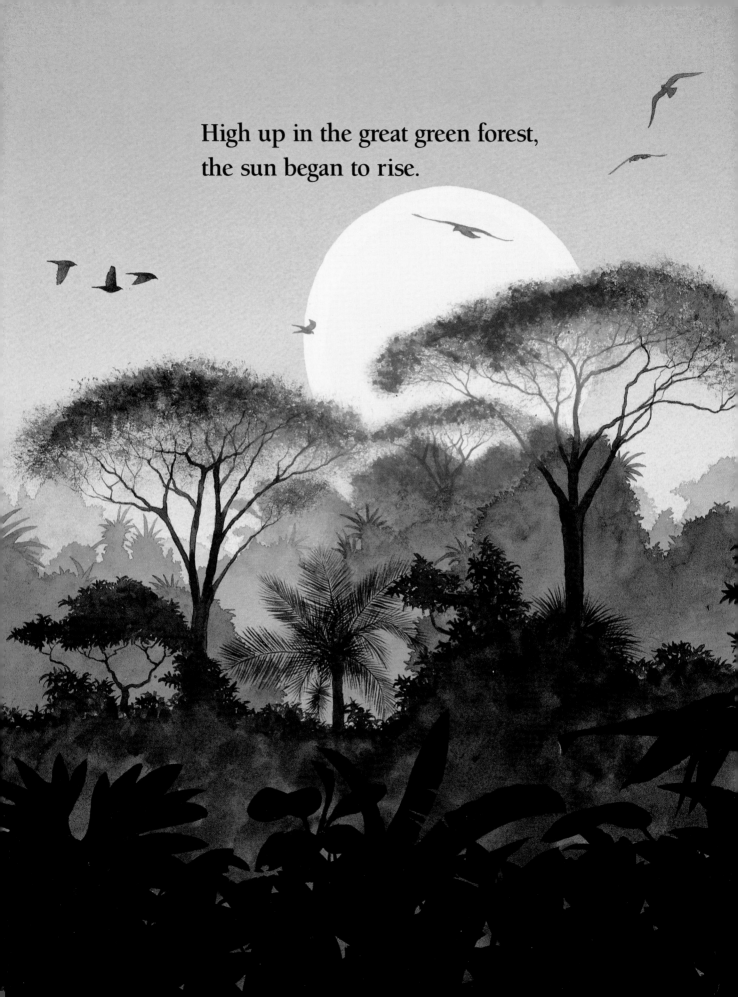

High up in the great green forest,
the sun began to rise.

Way down in the deep, dark shadows,
a tree mouse was curling up to sleep.

Creech! Creech! Woop! Woop!
chirped the frogs.

The sounds were screechy, the
sounds were sharp: *Woopoo!*
Woopoo! Creech! Creech!

"Stop that noise!" yelled the tree
mouse. "I'm trying to sleep!"

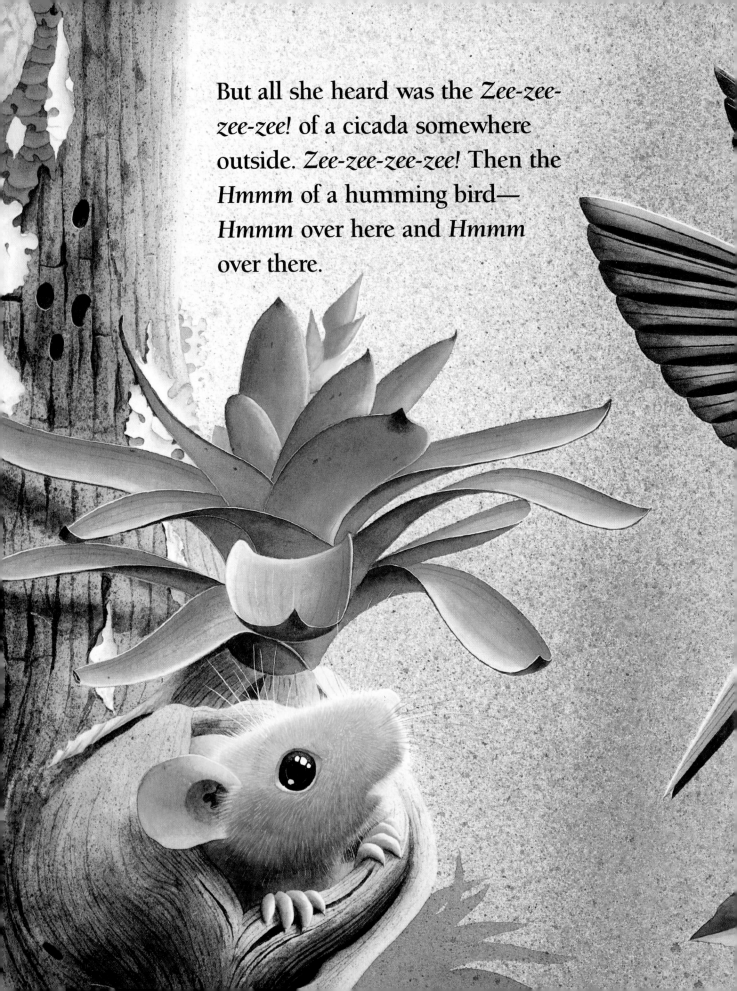

But all she heard was the *Zee-zee-zee-zee!* of a cicada somewhere outside. *Zee-zee-zee-zee!* Then the *Hmmm* of a humming bird— *Hmmm* over here and *Hmmm* over there.

"Stop that noise!" yelled the tree mouse. "I'm trying to sleep!"

Then *Keeoo…kedik-kedik-kedik!* came the calls from the forest crown.

Toucans pierced the curtain of green
with a *Keeoo…kedik-kedik-kedik!*

"Stop that noise!" yelled the tree mouse. "I'm trying to sleep!" But the forest was alive with songs and sounds.

Yaag! Screecha-screecha-screecha! squawked a macaw. *Yaag! SCRAAA! SCRAAA!* squawked another.

"Stop that noise!" yelled the tree mouse. "I'm trying to sleep!"

But her voice was drowned out by the monkeys that bickered in the branches. *Duwoop! Ooo-ooo-ooo-ooo!* whooped one. *Yeek! Yeek!* screamed the others.

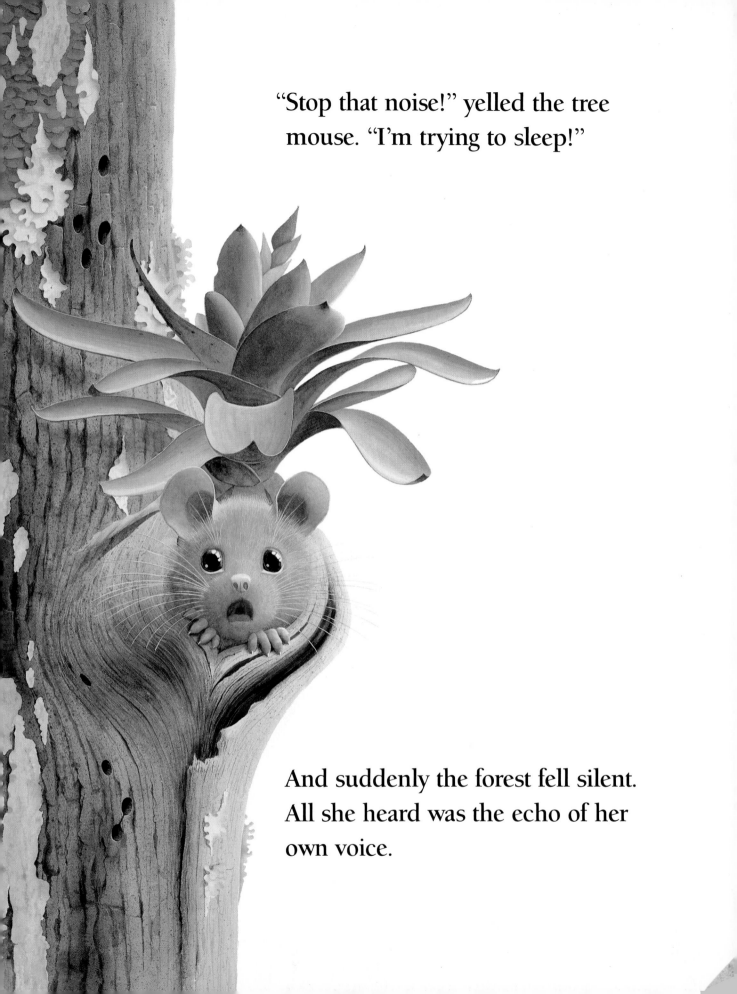

"Stop that noise!" yelled the tree mouse. "I'm trying to sleep!"

And suddenly the forest fell silent. All she heard was the echo of her own voice.

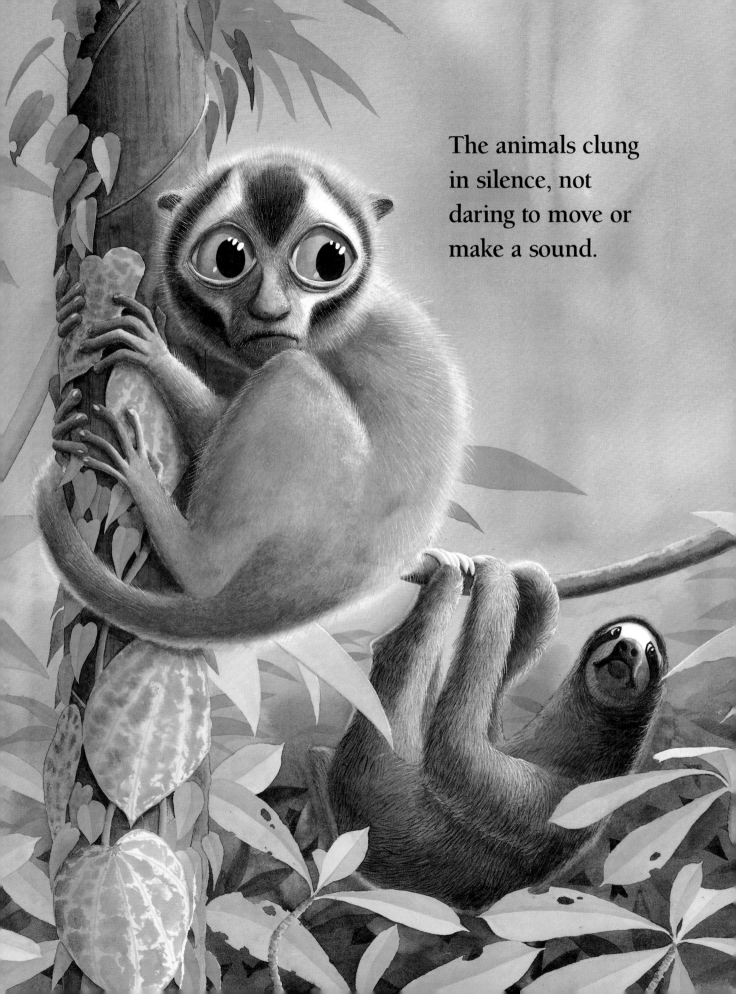

The animals clung in silence, not daring to move or make a sound.

Even the cats that ruled the forest now cowered in the quiet. That's better! thought the tree mouse.

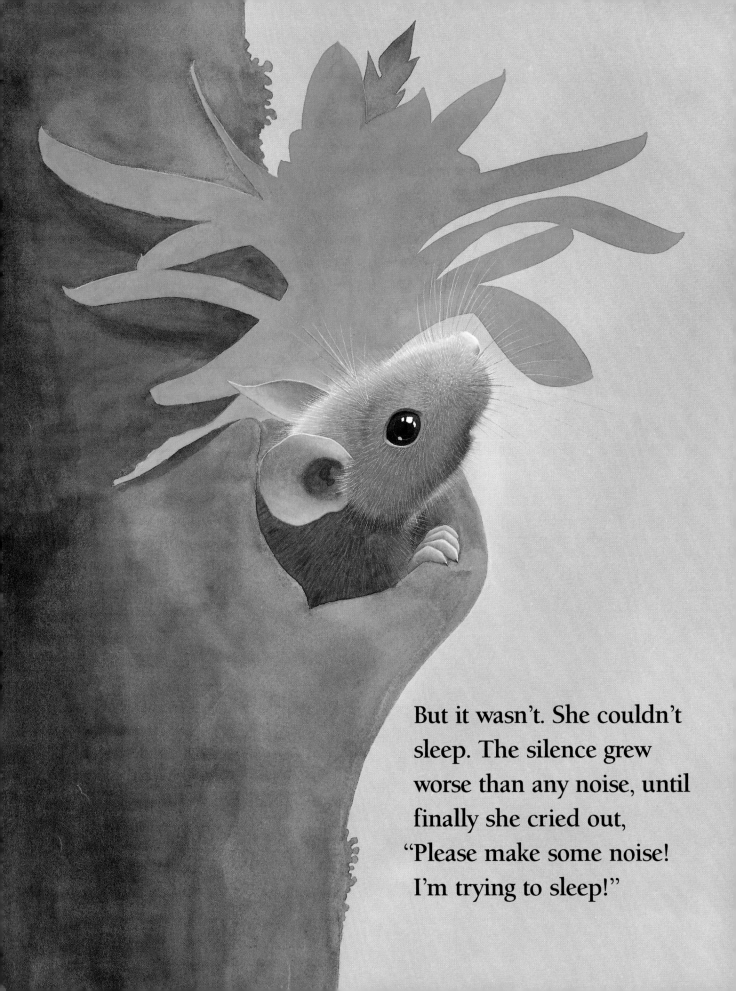

But it wasn't. She couldn't sleep. The silence grew worse than any noise, until finally she cried out, "Please make some noise! I'm trying to sleep!"

She waited. And then there was a noise. She
heard a distant *Brrrm, brrrm*…and then a
C-r-r-r-r-r-r-RACKA-DACKA-RACKA
SHOONG! that shook her to the ground.

A tree had fallen. And a gaping
hole was left in the crown of the
great green forest.

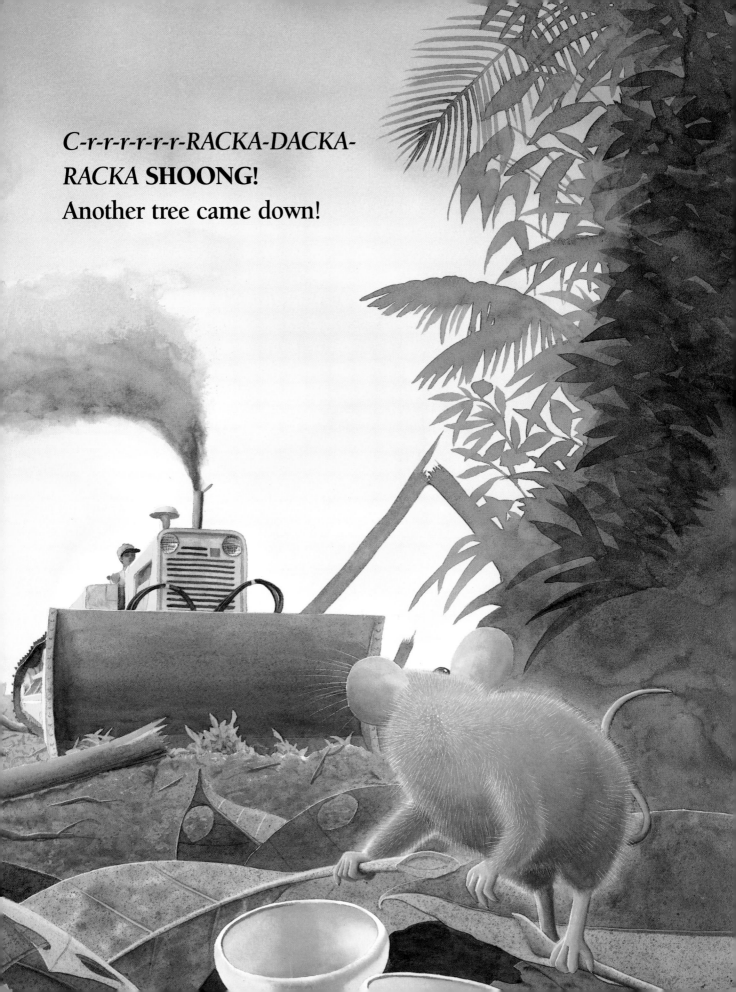

C-r-r-r-r-r-RACKA-DACKA-RACKA **SHOONG!**

Another tree came down!

Brrrm, BRRRM ... the ugly sound made the ground shudder. And the tree mouse knew her tree would be next.

She looked up at her home. Then she turned to the terrible sound. And at the top of her voice, she yelled, "STOP THAT NOISE!"

But that noise didn't stop.

Brrrm, it drew closer, *BRRRM,* till the earth thundered; *BRRRM!* it grew louder, **BRRRM!** till the earth shook. But the tree mouse stood firm.

And something made the driver stop. And when he stopped, he felt the silence. He saw the broken trees. He saw the fallen nests.

And he sensed angry eyes watching him.

So he sat and he thought. He stayed there
and thought till the sun went down. And
when it was dark, he went away.

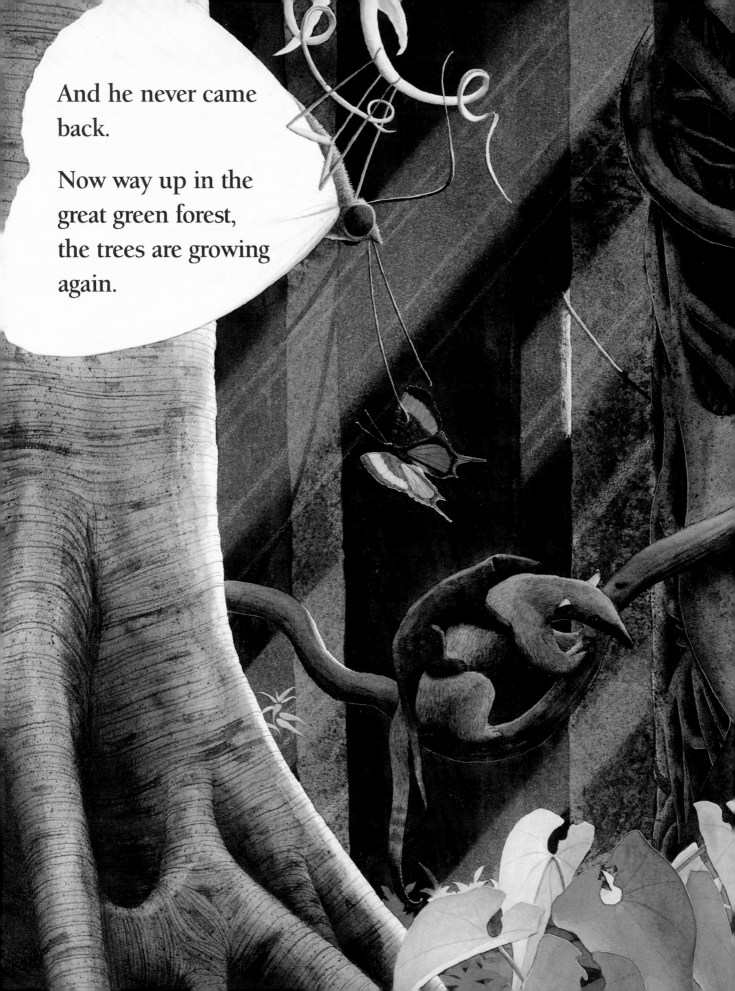

And he never came back.

Now way up in the great green forest, the trees are growing again.

And deep down in the dark shadows,
a tree mouse curls up and closes her
eyes. She listens to the songs and
sounds of the forest, which tell her
that, for now, she can sleep in peace.

For Extremely Tiny Most Miniature
and extremely tiny people everywhere

This edition is published by special arrangement with Crown Publishers, Inc.

Grateful acknowledgment is made to Crown Publishers, Inc. for permission to reprint *Stop That Noise!* by Paul Geraghty. Copyright © 1992 by Paul Geraghty.

Printed in Mexico

ISBN 0-15-302147-0

4 5 6 7 8 9 10   050   97 96 95